SIMON SPOTLIGHT & NICKELODEON PRESENT:

GO DiEGO GO!

· EXTREME RESCUE ·

DOLPHIN MISSION

| ERICA DAVID | WARNER MCGEE |
| writer | artist |

| line look by NICK SCIACCA | SIOBHAN CIMINERA editor | CHRISTINE J. MARSHALL managing editor |

 SIMON SPOTLIGHT/NICKELODEON NEW YORK   LONDON   TORONTO   SYDNEY

BASED ON THE TV SERIES *GO, DIEGO, GO!*™ AS SEEN ON NICK JR.®

SIMON SPOTLIGHT
AN IMPRINT OF SIMON & SCHUSTER CHILDREN'S PUBLISHING DIVISION
1230 AVENUE OF THE AMERICAS, NEW YORK, NEW YORK 10020
© 2009 VIACOM INTERNATIONAL INC. ALL RIGHTS RESERVED. NICK JR., *GO, DIEGO, GO!*, AND ALL RELATED TITLES, LOGOS, AND CHARACTERS ARE
TRADEMARKS OF VIACOM INTERNATIONAL INC. ALL RIGHTS RESERVED, INCLUDING THE RIGHT OF REPRODUCTION IN WHOLE OR IN PART IN ANY FORM.
SIMON SPOTLIGHT AND COLOPHON ARE REGISTERED TRADEMARKS OF SIMON & SCHUSTER, INC. MANUFACTURED IN THE UNITED STATES OF AMERICA
FIRST EDITION 2 4 6 8 10 9 7 5 3 1
ISBN: 978-1-4169-7825-1

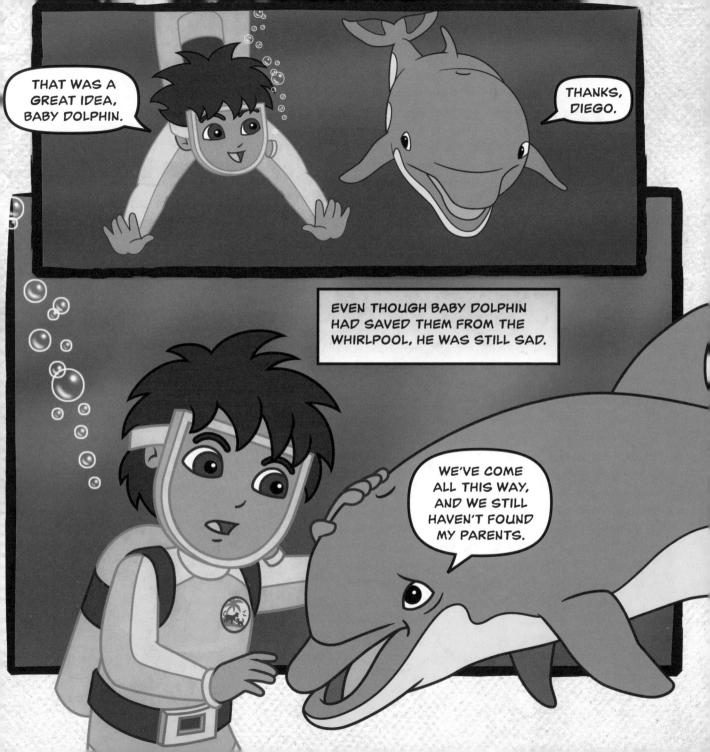

BABY DOLPHIN'S CALL TRAVELED
ACROSS THE OCEAN . . .